The Wrong Fairy Tale

JACK
and the Three Bears

First American Edition 2021
Kane Miller, A Division of EDC Publishing

A Raspberry Book
Art direction and cover design: Sidonie Beresford-Browne
Internal design: Sidonie Beresford-Browne & Ailsa Cullen
Copyright © Raspberry Books Ltd 2020

For information contact:
Kane Miller, A Division of EDC Publishing
P.O. Box 470663,
Tulsa, OK 74147-0663
www.kanemiller.com
www.usbornebooksandmore.com

Library of Congress Control Number: 2020936348
Printed in China
ISBN: 978-1-68464-161-1
2 3 4 5 6 7 8 9 10

The Wrong Fairy Tale

By Tracey Turner
and Summer Macon

JACK
and the Three Bears

Kane Miller
A DIVISION OF EDC PUBLISHING

Once upon a time in the Land of Fairy Tales, Mommy Bear, Daddy Bear, and Baby Bear went out for a walk while they waited for their porridge to cool down.

MAMA BEAR'S SHED

TRESPASSERS WILL BE CHASED AWAY

They hadn't gone far when . . .
"Good grief!" exclaimed Daddy Bear. "I'm sure
that wasn't there the last time I looked."

"It's a gigantic beanstalk," said Mommy Bear.

"It must be magic!" cried Baby Bear excitedly.

Before Mommy Bear and Daddy Bear could stop him, the small bear was clambering up the beanstalk surprisingly quickly.

"COME BACK!"

they shouted.

But they could only see Baby Bear's stout, furry legs far above them. With a sigh, Mommy Bear and Daddy Bear began to climb after him.

Meanwhile, Jack was making his third visit
to the castle at the top of the beanstalk.

Once again, he congratulated himself
for swapping Daisy the cow for
a handful of magic beans.

On his first visit, Jack had discovered the castle and its fabulous treasures. He'd climbed back down to surprise his mother with a bagful of golden coins.

The second time, he'd taken a magic harp that played and sang by itself.

This time, Jack was planning to make off with a white hen. But not just any old white hen—this one laid golden eggs. Jack and his mother would never go hungry again!

GOLDIE

There was just one problem. And it was quite a **big** problem . . .

THUMP

THUMP

It turned out that the Giant did not like boys stealing golden coins and magic harps from his castle. Both times, Jack had only just managed to get away.

It sounded very much as though the Giant was after him **right now**.

THUMP!

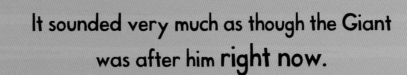

Jack clutched the white hen tightly as he dashed through the castle. The footsteps were getting closer.

As Jack skidded into the castle kitchen he bumped into something hairy . . .

"Who are you?" said Baby Bear in a loud voice. "And what's that thumping noise? Is there an elephant on the loose?"

THUMP!!

THUMP!

SHHH!

THUMP!

"Shhhhh!" said Jack. "I'm Jack, and that sound is a ferocious giant! Quick! In here!"

THUMP!

BAKING SODA

Jack pulled Baby Bear into the kitchen pantry and shut the door.

PANT

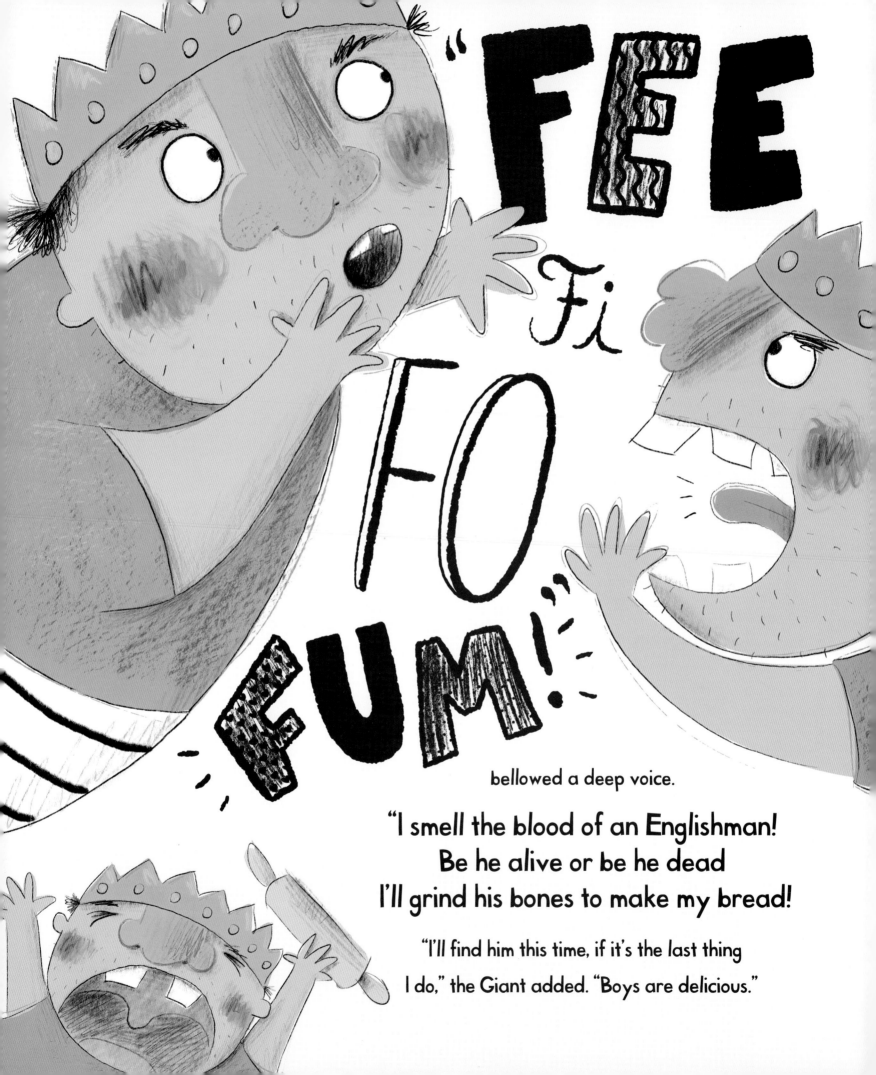

"FEE Fi FO FUM!"

bellowed a deep voice.

"I smell the blood of an Englishman!
Be he alive or be he dead
I'll grind his bones to make my bread!

"I'll find him this time, if it's the last thing
I do," the Giant added. "Boys are delicious."

Meanwhile, Mommy
Bear and Daddy Bear
had made it up
the beanstalk.

ARTISAN BREAD
ROLLS 'N MORE
YUMMY!
YOU CAN BAKE

"The castle kitchen!" said Mommy Bear.
"What's that thumping noise?" said Daddy
Bear. "Sounds like an elephant."

"Quick, in here!" said Baby Bear from the pantry
as the Giant's footsteps sounded closer still.
"Who are you?" Daddy Bear asked Jack.
"And why are you clutching a hen?"
added Mommy Bear.

BONE
BREAD:

YUM!

S

"Shhhhh!" said
Jack and Baby
Bear together.

"Today is full of surprises!" whispered Mommy Bear, inside the pantry. "We only went for a walk while our breakfast cooled down."
"Hang on," said Jack, "were you having porridge for breakfast?"
The Three Bears nodded.

Three bears go for a walk while their porridge cools . . .

A boy called Jack climbs a beanstalk . . .
"YOU'RE IN THE WRONG FAiRY TALE!"

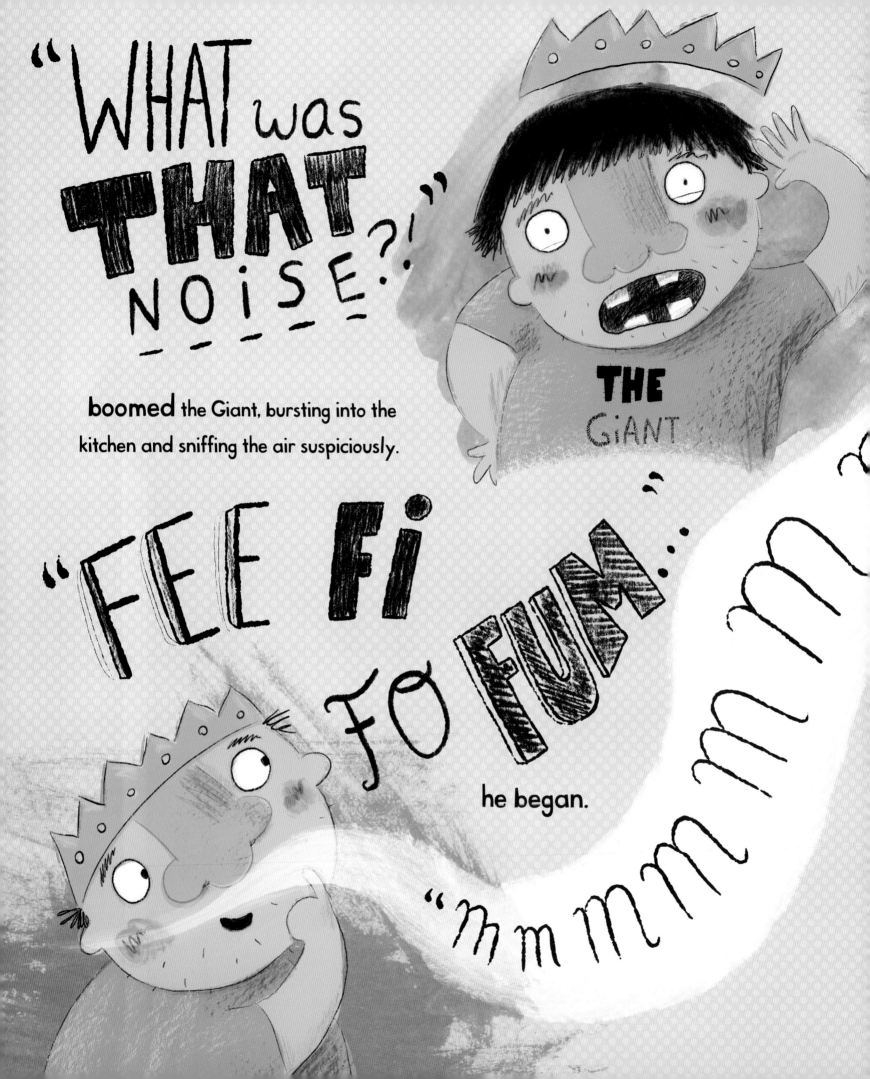

SAUSAGES.

Maybe that's what I could smell all along."

THE GiANT

MUNCH SLURP!

THE

PANTRY

In the pantry, Jack and the Three Bears were holding their breath.

CRUNCH!!!

After what seemed like a very long time
listening to the Giant eating sausages,
Jack and the Three Bears heard a **big** yawn.

Then a sort of snuffling sound.
Then an **enormous** snore.
The snores got **louder** and **louder**.

"I can hardly hear myself think!" said Mommy Bear.

"Let's make a run for it," said Jack.

PANTRY

Daddy Bear was just closing the kitchen door v-e-r-y q-u-i-e-t-l-y behind them, when . . .

"PERCAW!"

clucked the hen.

GOLDIE

"Cluck cluck cluck percaw!"
Jack and the Three Bears froze.

The snoring stopped.

"What's that?" bellowed the Giant. "Is that you, Goldie? Who's there?"

"Come on!" cried Jack, grabbing Baby Bear's paw. The four of them sprinted along the path and began to clamber quickly down the beanstalk.

"FEE FI FO FUM!"

thundered the Giant as he opened the kitchen door.

Jack chopped frantically at
the beanstalk with the axe.
"Come on, Jack!" said Daddy Bear.

"Fee fi fo fum!"

"He's getting closer!" said Baby Bear
with a squeak in his voice.

"Fee fi fo–"
But the Giant's voice was drowned
out by a loud roar.

It was a **lot** quicker with the chainsaw.
With a mighty **whump!** the beanstalk fell.

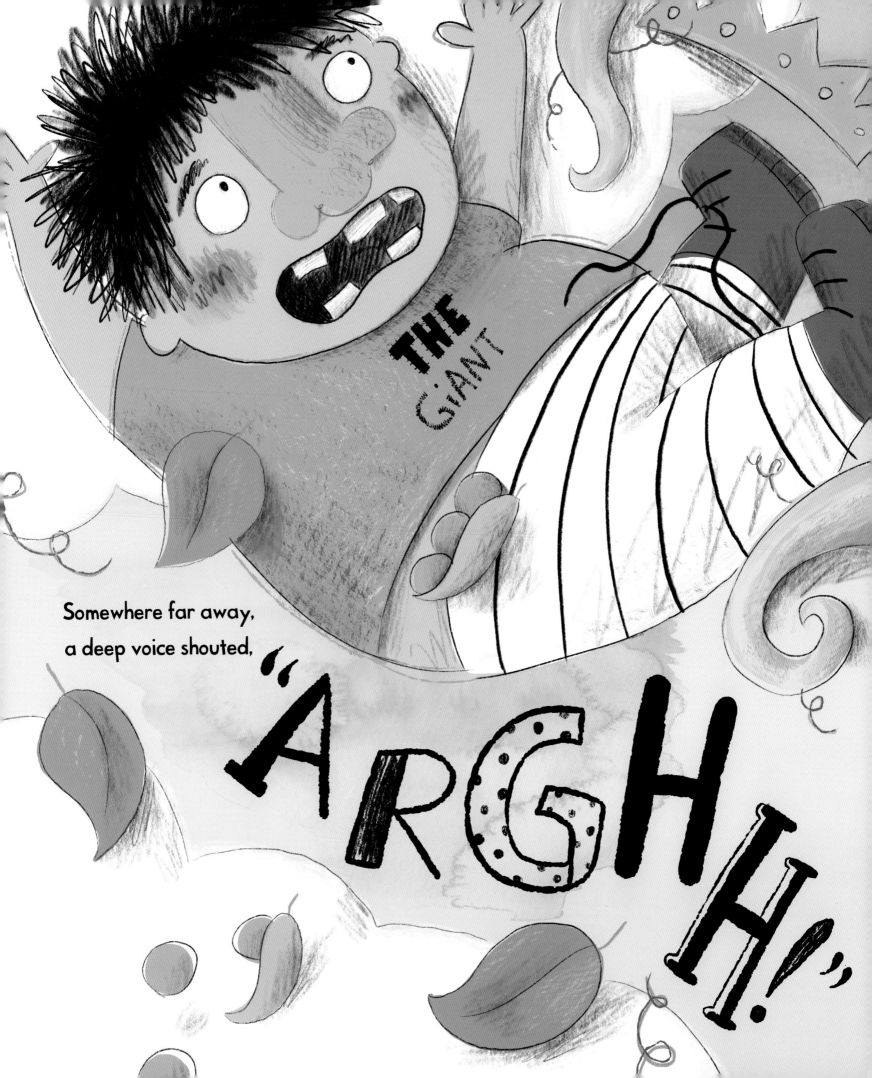

THE GIANT

Somewhere far away,
a deep voice shouted,
"ARGHH!"

That was the last anyone ever saw of the Giant.
The white hen proved to be a very good
layer of golden eggs. Jack and his mother
never did go hungry again.

Jack and the Three Bears used some of the gold to start a very successful business.

And they all lived happily ever after.

GOLDEN PORRIDGE CO.

GOLDEN OATS

Even though it was completely
the WRONG FAIRY TALE.

THE END